YOU BE
THE JURY
Courtroom III

Also by Marvin Miller:

YOU BE THE JURY
YOU BE THE JURY: COURTROOM II

YOU BE THE JURY
Courtroom III

Marvin Miller

Illustrated by Bob Roper

SCHOLASTIC INC.
New York Toronto London Auckland Sydney

. . for Robby, again . . . .

All names used in this book are fictional, and any resemblance to persons living or dead is purely coincidental.

No part of this publication may be reproduced in whole or in part, or stored in a retrieval system, or transmitted in any form or by any means, electronic, mechanical, photocopying, recording, or otherwise, without written permission of the publisher. For information regarding permission, write to Scholastic Inc., 730 Broadway, New York, NY 10003.

ISBN 0-590-43048-3

Copyright © 1990 by Marvin Miller. All rights reserved. Published by Scholastic Inc.

12 11 10 9 8 7 6 5 4 3   0 1 2 3 4 5/9

Printed in the U.S.A.   40
First Scholastic printing, January 1990

CONTENTS

Order in the Court

Ladies and Gentlemen of the Jury:

This court is now in session. My name is Judge John Dennenberg. You are the jury, and the trials are set to begin.

You have a serious responsibility. Will the innocent be sent to jail and the guilty go free? Let's hope not. Your job is to make sure that justice is served.

Read each case carefully. Study the evidence presented and then decide.

GUILTY OR NOT GUILTY??

Both sides of the case will be presented to you. The person who has the complaint is called the *plaintiff*. He or she has brought the case to court. If a crime is involved, the State is the accuser.

The person being accused is called the *defendant*. The defendant is pleading his or her innocence and presents a much different version of what happened.

IN EACH CASE, THREE PIECES OF EVIDENCE WILL BE PRESENTED AS

1

EXHIBITS A, B, AND C. EXAMINE THE EXHIBITS VERY CAREFULLY. A *CLUE* TO THE SOLUTION OF EACH CASE WILL BE FOUND THERE. IT WILL DIRECTLY POINT TO THE INNOCENCE OR GUILT OF THE ACCUSED.

Remember, each side will try to convince you that his or her version is what actually happened. BUT YOU MUST MAKE THE FINAL DECISION.

The Case of the Burning Barn

LADIES AND GENTLEMEN OF THE JURY:

When a fire occurs, and there is reason to believe it was purposely set to collect insurance, payment can be denied.

Today you are in court to decide on this issue.

Ezra Stiles, the plaintiff, is suing Oxford Insurance Company to collect insurance money for his barn, which was destroyed by fire. The company refuses to pay the claim. The insurance company's attorney thinks Mr. Stiles started the fire on purpose.

Ezra Stiles has given the following testimony:

"It was late in the evening of May 14. I've been a farmer all my life so I generally go to bed pretty early. All at once I heard this knocking on my door. I was half asleep by then and at first I thought I was just dreaming. When the knocking continued, I got up.

"I quickly threw on some clothes and ran downstairs. When I opened the door, there was Officer Conrad Darnoc. He told me he'd been driving by

3

and seen flames coming from a window in my barn. He radioed for help and drove to the barn. There's a water spigot there, but he couldn't find a hose, so he drove up to the house to get help.

"Well, I grabbed the hose from my porch and we drove to my barn. By that time the fire had spread across one side of the barn. It was completely in flames."

EXHIBIT A is a photograph taken after the fire truck arrived.

Ezra Stiles is suing Oxford Insurance for $11,000, the cost of his barn. But the insurance company labels the blaze as suspicious.

The plaintiff thinks the insurance company is trying to avoid paying him. He believes the fire was set by a drifter who was seen in the area.

Mr. Stiles offers as proof EXHIBIT B, a report received by police several days earlier. It is a neighbor's complaint of a stranger who was seen wandering around the area the week of the fire.

Ezra Stiles continued his testimony:

"The day before the fire I found a few cigarette butts near my barn. There were also some empty food cans. I couldn't figure out how they got there."

The plaintiff claims the stranger may have used his barn as a place to sleep. He could have accidentally started the fire with a cigarette.

A lawyer for Oxford Insurance Company believes Stiles's actions at the time of the fire were very suspicious. They called Officer Darnoc to

4

testify. First the question and then his answer:

Q: What did you do when you saw the fire?

A: I drove up the hill to Ezra Stiles's house. I thought I could use his hose until the fire truck arrived.

Q: How long did it take him to come to the door?

A: It was quite a while. I knocked and knocked, yelling for him to open the door. But there was no answer. I shouted and knocked for several minutes. Finally Stiles came to the door.

Q: What did he say when you told him about the fire?

A: Stiles was half dressed and he was rubbing his eyes. He said he had been sleeping.

The insurance company's lawyers claim a different reason Ezra Stiles took so long to answer the door. They believe he set the barn fire himself.

They claim that the farmer was down by his barn, spreading the fire, when he saw the policeman's car approaching. Under cover of darkness, he ran up a back road to his house, entered through the rear, and then opened the front door for Officer Darnoc.

The company's lawyers offer further proof in EXHIBIT C. It is a picture of the door of the barn. You will note that a wooden bar keeps the door closed.

If a stranger had accidentally started the fire inside the barn, he never would have bothered to lock the door before he fled.

The lawyers claim that Ezra Stiles had a good reason to start the fire. He recently had retired from farming. The barn was of little use to him.

Oxford Insurance Company believes the farmer set the fire as a means of collecting insurance money for a building that was no longer needed.

LADIES AND GENTLEMEN OF THE JURY:

You have just heard the Case of the Burning Barn. You must decide the merits of Ezra Stiles's claim. Be sure to carefully examine the evidence in EXHIBITS A, B, and C.

Was the barn fire started by a stranger? Or did the farmer start it to collect insurance money?

EXHIBIT B

D.D.5

CRIME CLASSIFICATION	POLICE DEPARTMENT REPORT
SUSPICIOUS PERSON	

NAME OF COMPLAINANT	ADDRESS
BETTY MARGATE	712 CHESTNUT ROAD

May 10, 1989
7:46 am phone call. Complainant observed a stranger walking down Chestnut Road, carrying a shopping bag filled with clothing. A blanket was draped around his shoulders.

Stranger was male, 6ft tall and wearing dungarees and a blue baseball cap.

Greg Banon

OFFICER ON DUTY

EXHIBIT C

VERDICT

THE FIRE WAS STARTED TO COLLECT
INSURANCE MONEY.

In his testimony, the farmer said that when he
was awakened, he quickly threw on some clothes
and ran downstairs. EXHIBIT A shows Stiles at
his barn half dressed. But his high boots are laced
up.

If he had hurried to answer the door, he would
not have had time to lace them.

While Ezra Stiles was setting the fire, he
spotted Officer Darnoc. He quickly ran back to
his house and threw *off* some clothes to make it
look as though he had been sleeping.
But he forgot to unlace his boots.

The Case of
the Jelly Bean Jubilee

LADIES AND GENTLEMEN OF THE JURY:

When someone wins a contest by cheating, he or she is not entitled to keep the prize.

That is the point of law you must keep in mind today, as you decide to whom a contest prize rightfully belongs.

Curt Barr, the plaintiff, is suing Wendy Darling, the defendant, for the prize of a TV set. He claims she won it by cheating. But Wendy Darling says she won the prize fair and square.

Mr. Noel Roxy has testified as follows on behalf of the plaintiff:

"I'm Noel Roxy. That's right, the one and only Noel Roxy, owner of the fabulous Roxy Movie Palace. You've heard our slogan — 'Come to the Roxy, where everyone's a star!'

"During the week of October 18, we held a contest to advertise our fabulous new movie, *Jack and the Jelly Beanstalk*. We decided to call our contest the Jelly Bean Jubilee."

In the lobby of the theater was a large jar holding hundreds of jelly beans. The theater offered a TV

11

to the person who most closely guessed the number of jelly beans in the jar.

The contest drew a large crowd. On the final day of the movie, the contest winner was announced.

When Noel Roxy opened the ballots, he was surprised to find that there were two winners. The jar held exactly 1,700 jelly beans. Wendy Darling guessed there were 1,750 in the jar. Curt Barr's guess was 1,650.

Since both persons were equally close, Mr. Roxy announced a playoff.

He had another bean jar in his office. He would bring it on the stage the next day. Each would guess the number of jelly beans inside the new jar. The winner of the tiebreaker would get the TV.

The day of the tiebreaker, both winners were called on stage. To everyone's amazement, Wendy Darling guessed the exact number of jelly beans in the jar — 2,240. Curt Barr's guess was far off.

Barr was disappointed. After the movie, he met the theater owner in the lobby. Mr. Roxy invited the young man to his second floor office for a recount.

When they entered the office, Curt Barr noticed that the window was open and an outside ladder was leaning against the sill.

Mr. Roxy was shocked. Someone had used the ladder to get into his office.

Curt Barr, the plaintiff, claims it could only have been Wendy Darling. He says she must have sneaked into the office the morning of the tie-breaker and counted the jelly beans ahead of time.

EXHIBIT A is a photograph of the office as it appeared when Barr and Roxy entered it.

I will read from the testimony of Noel Roxy. First the question and then his answer:

Q: Could anyone walk into your office while the second jelly bean jar was there?

A: That was impossible. I'm the only one with a key. The contest drew a lot of publicity, so I carefully locked the door each time I left the office.

Q: Had you kept your window locked, too?

A: I'm not sure. The window was definitely closed. But I'm not sure if it was locked.

Q: When you went into your office to bring the jelly bean jar to the stage, was the ladder leaning against the open window?

A: I didn't notice. But it must have been there.

Q: Did you lock your office door when you brought the jar to the stage?

A: No. There was no need to. I had the jar.

Q: Can you identify the ladder?

A: Yes. It's the one we keep in a checkroom in our lobby.

As further proof that Wendy Darling cheated, the plaintiff has entered this additional photo-

13

graph of the office as EXHIBIT B. He calls your attention to the stool near the bookcase. The bookshelf where Noel Roxy kept the second jelly bean jar is marked with an "X."

Ms. Darling was too short to reach the jar. Curt Barr contends that she moved the stool over to the bookshelf to reach the jar.

But afterwards, she forgot to remove the accusing evidence — the stool.

Wendy Darling insists that she didn't cheat. She says she won the TV set honestly and refuses to give it back.

She says the ladder was put in the window by Barr to make it look like she broke into the office. Everyone knew that he was upset when he lost the contest.

Ms. Darling suggested another version of what happened:

"I think Curt Barr planted the ladder and stool to make it look like I cheated. He thought he could get away with it. He thought no one would believe I guessed the exact number of jelly beans."

She claims that after Barr lost the tiebreaker, he took the ladder from the theater's checkroom and carried it up to the owner's office. Then he dropped it from the window to the ground. It looked like someone had climbed up the ladder and into the office.

As proof of her claim, Ms. Darling showed EXHIBIT C, a photograph of the back stairs door leading from the checkroom to the owner's office. Barr could have carried the ladder upstairs without being seen.

LADIES AND GENTLEMEN OF THE JURY:
You have just heard the Case of the Jelly Bean Jubilee. You must decide the merits of Curt Barr's claim. Be sure to carefully examine the evidence in EXHIBITS A, B, and C.

Did Wendy Darling secretly climb into the office and count the jelly beans? Or was the ladder placed there by Barr after he lost the contest?

EXHIBIT C

VERDICT

THE LADDER WAS PLACED IN THE WINDOW AFTER THE CONTEST.

EXHIBIT A shows the ladder in Mr. Roxy's window. Notice that the window swings outwards. It would have been impossible for Wendy Darling to lean an outside ladder against the windowsill and climb up it. The top of the ladder would have prevented the window from opening.

After the tiebreaker, Curt Barr carried a ladder up to the office, opened the window, and slipped it outside, leaning one end against the sill.

The Case of
the Sports Superstar

LADIES AND GENTLEMEN OF THE JURY:

When a person's picture is used in an advertisement without permission, even if that person is a famous public figure, it is an invasion of that person's privacy.

Such is the case before you today.

Byron "Lefty" Ward, the plaintiff, was once the leading pitcher in the National Baseball League. He is suing TV station KBB for illegally using his name and picture to advertise a TV sports event. KBB, the defendant, claims they used Ward's picture with the star's permission.

Wink Hastings of TV station KBB has testified as follows:

"Wink Hastings is my name and TV is my game. I'm the station manager at KBB.

"When KBB got the rights to televise Weston College baseball games, we wanted to attract as many viewers as possible. Then one morning, I got this brilliant idea. They don't call me 'Quick-as-a-

Wink' Hastings for nothing. I realized that if we could hire Byron Ward as our announcer, more people would watch the games."

Hastings met with Ward. The baseball star said he was very interested. Byron Ward signed a letter of agreement stating he would accept the job if the TV station could work out an agreeable contract.

This letter was entered as EXHIBIT A.

During their next meeting, the two men argued over the terms of the agreement. Wink Hastings was under pressure. The day of the first game was approaching. KBB had to begin its advertising campaign.

Byron Ward finally walked out of the talks, stating he had changed his mind. He didn't want to work for KBB. But by that time the advertisement with Ward's picture was in newspapers. It said he was announcing the games.

Byron Ward claims the advertisement damaged his reputation. His fans expected to see him as announcer and they were disappointed.

Byron Ward testified about his dealings with Wink Hastings and KBB. First the question and then his answer:

Q: Is this your signature on the letter?
A: Yes, it is. But Mr. Hastings knew I would announce the games only if he met my terms.

The wording in the letter says so.

Q: Why didn't you take the job?

A: I didn't like Hastings's attitude. First he told me he would pay me a lot of money. Later he changed his mind. I got so disgusted that I told him I didn't want to work for his TV station.

Q: Did you pose for the picture in the ad and give KBB permission to use it?

A: No, I certainly did not.

EXHIBIT B is the advertisement that is the reason for Byron Ward's legal action against KBB. It is a photograph of Byron Ward seated behind a KBB microphone.

Wink Hastings told the court a completely different story:

"When I first suggested the announcing job to Ward, he was very interested.

"I told him we needed to prepare an advertising campaign immediately and he agreed to pose for it. We had his permission.

"But when it got down to details, Ward became unreasonable. Besides wanting a higher salary, he insisted we buy him a new wardrobe. He wanted a different suit for every game. He also said he needed a private dressing room.

"We just couldn't afford his demands. By the time we decided we couldn't work things out, it was too late to stop the advertisement."

Byron Ward states that the station manager is lying. He claims that the picture in the advertisement is a complete fake. He never posed for it.

Ward claims that since KBB needed to prepare the ad before they had a final agreement, someone else posed behind a KBB microphone. Then the artist glued on a photograph of the celebrity's head.

To prove his accusation, Ward explained to the court how he thinks the photograph was made:

"They cut out my head from a photograph taken when I was still playing baseball. Then they glued it onto a photograph of someone else."

Mr. Ward showed the court EXHIBIT C. He believes this is the photograph the artist used to create the picture of him sitting at the mike.

Byron Ward continued his testimony:

"Notice the similarities between my face on the picture in uniform and my face in the ad. KBB eliminated the lock of hair hanging down my forehead. They knew announcers had to have a neater look.

"I never posed for the advertisement. It's an obvious phony, made up from my photograph."

LADIES AND GENTLEMEN OF THE JURY:
You have just heard the Case of the Sports

Superstar. You must decide the merits of Mr. Ward's claim. Be sure to carefully examine the evidence in EXHIBITS A, B, and C.

Was the advertisement for KBB prepared with Byron Ward's permission? Or did the TV station use a fake ad?

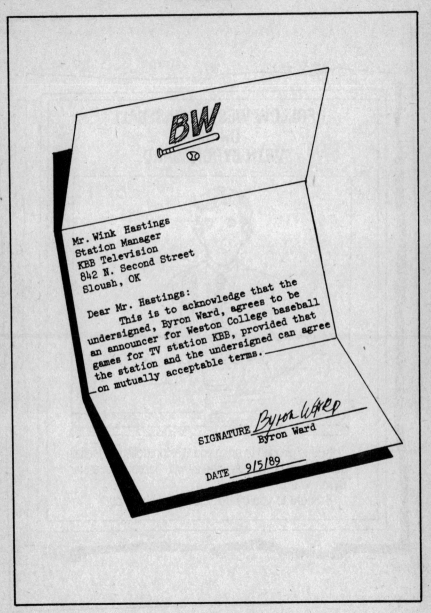

Mr. Wink Hastings
Station Manager
KBB Television
842 N. Second Street
Sloush, OK

Dear Mr. Hastings:

This is to acknowledge that the undersigned, Byron Ward, agrees to be an announcer for Weston College baseball games for TV station KBB, provided that the station and the undersigned can agree on mutually acceptable terms.

SIGNATURE _Byron Ward_
Byron Ward

DATE _9/5/89_

FOLLOW WESTON BASEBALL ON KBB WITH BYRON WARD

KBB is pleased to bring you Weston College baseball games. Follow the play-by-play with baseball superstar Byron Ward.

Brought to you by BUZZ OFF Roach Spray.

EXHIBIT C

VERDICT

THE ADVERTISEMENT WAS A FAKE.

EXHIBIT C shows Byron Ward wearing a *left-handed* baseball glove (on his right hand). And Ward's signature on the letter in EXHIBIT A has a slant often seen in the penmanship of left-handed writers. So Byron Ward *was a lefty*. But the advertisement in EXHIBIT B shows a photo of Ward writing with his *right* hand. Byron "Lefty" Ward never posed for the ad.

The Case of
the Disappearing Shopper

Ladies AND GENTLEMEN OF THE JURY:

Shoplifting is the act of taking merchandise from a store without paying for it. The store must have proof the person intended to steal the property.

Keep this issue of proof in mind as you examine the case before you today.

Flash Appliances, the plaintiff, accuses Donald Hill, the defendant, of shoplifting a stereo-radio from its store. Hill claims he is innocent and carried the radio out of the store to help a stranger. He says the stranger had tricked him.

Benjamin Gunn, a store guard, has testified as follows:

"My name is Ben Gunn, and I'm a security guard at Flash Appliances. Saturday, July 8, was a busy shopping day for us. It was raining, and the bad weather kept people indoors.

"At approximately 3:10 P.M., there was a bright flash of lightning followed by a loud thunderclap. All the store's lights went out.

"You can't be too careful when the power goes

out. That's why I moved to the front of the store and stood by the exit door.

"When the lights came back on, I saw this boxed radio by the door. I figured that while the lights were out, someone took the radio from a shelf, carried it past the cashier's counter, and put it in a convenient place where it could be taken out without paying.

"Then the rain stopped. No one touched the radio at first. But then, about ten minutes later, I saw this man, Donald Hill, pick up the box and carry it out to the parking lot. I stopped him just before he got to his car and held him there until the police arrived."

EXHIBIT A is a photograph of the two men, taken after the police arrived. They are standing next to Hill's car.

Mr. Hill insists he was not in the store when the lights went out. He testified as follows:

"I live about a mile from Flash. When the rain stopped, I wanted to go jogging. But my Walkman needed new batteries. So I drove over to the store to get some.

"I pulled into a parking space. A woman had just left the store and was carrying packages to her car. It was next to mine.

"She had trouble holding the packages and finding the car keys in her purse. I asked if she needed help.

"The lady told me she could manage, but she

had left a package by the exit door. She said I could save her a trip if I would bring it out.

"That's when I went into the store and walked over to the exit door. I picked up the box and carried it outside.

"When I looked for her car, the woman was gone. All of a sudden the guard stopped me."

Lawyers for the store challenged Donald Hill's story. First their question and then Hill's answer:

Q: Didn't it seem strange that there was no store sticker on the box you took, to show the merchandise was paid for?

A: I never really noticed. I was only trying to do a good deed.

Q: Did the other packages the woman carried to her car have paid stickers on them?

A: I remember seeing them. They're so big it's hard to miss.

Q: How can you account for the woman's disappearance?

A: I guess she saw the store guard following me and knew she would be caught. So she just drove away.

The store's lawyers entered as EXHIBIT B a sample of a "paid" sticker on an appliance box. The store uses these stickers as security so they know when merchandise has been paid for.

The store's lawyers went on to say that the

police have been unable to locate the person whom Hill says he was helping. The lawyers claim there never was such a person.

Donald Hill's lawyer stated that the woman was the one who committed the crime. She tricked Hill into carrying out the radio.

Hill's lawyer further claimed that the store lacks sufficient proof. Since the radio was moved while the lights were out, Flash Appliances must prove Mr. Hill was in the store at the time.

Hill's attorney showed EXHIBIT C, a diagram of the front of the store. The entrance door is very close to the exit door. EXHIBIT C shows that it was possible for Donald Hill to walk through the entrance door after the lights went back on and go directly to the exit door. He could have done this without being seen by the guard.

LADIES AND GENTLEMEN OF THE JURY:
You have just heard the Case of the Disappearing Shopper. You must decide the merits of Flash Appliances's claim. Be sure to carefully examine the evidence in EXHIBITS A, B, and C.

Was Donald Hill tricked into taking the stereo-radio? Or did he steal it?

EXHIBIT A

EXHIBIT B

EXHIBIT C

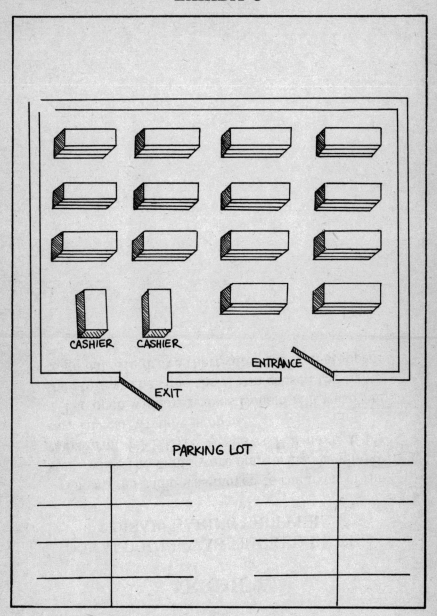

VERDICT

**DONALD HILL WAS TRICKED BY THE
DISAPPEARING SHOPPER.**

The stereo-radio was moved to the front of the
store while the lights were out during the all-day
rainstorm. EXHIBIT A shows Hill next to his
car. His car window is open.

The open window proves Donald Hill wasn't in
the store at the time the storm caused the lights
to go out. He drove there after the rain stopped.

The Case of
the Squished Tomatoes

LADIES AND GENTLEMEN OF THE JURY:

If a burglary takes place, and a great deal of money is stolen, the thief may be sent to prison for a very long time.

Carefully consider this serious penalty as you listen to the evidence presented here today.

Since we are in criminal court today, the State is the accuser. The State accuses Andrew Turner, the defendant, of stealing $2,000 from the safe of the Hopp-n-Shop Grocery Store. Andrew Turner, who works at Hopp-n-Shop, insists he is innocent.

The State called Harvey Hopp as its first witness.

"My name is Harvey Hopp. I own the Hopp-n-Shop Grocery Store. On the evening of June 5, at approximately 9:15 P.M., I locked up the store for the night and headed home. I learned later that at 9:56 P.M., the burglar alarm for the store's safe went off. Luckily the police responded immediately."

EXHIBIT A is an official record of the burglar alarm report.

When the police arrived, they discovered that

the back door of the store was unlocked. In searching the store, they found the office safe open. The money inside had been stolen.

In a corner of the store, near a vegetable bin, police found a basket of spilled tomatoes.

The thief had left his mark. Damaged tomatoes, some half eaten, were on the floor. On a large wall mirror, scrawled in the juice of a squished tomato, the thief had written the word "DELICIOUS!"

EXHIBIT B is a photograph of the damage done by the thief.

The State questioned Harvey Hopp further. First the question and then his answer:

Q: Are you positive you locked the front and back door of the store on the evening of the burglary?

A: I'm certain I did. I've followed the same routine for years.

Q: Did anyone have the combination to your safe?

A: I'm the only one. But it's possible that someone who worked for me could have seen me open the safe and remembered the combination.

Q: Does anyone else use your office?

A: No. I'm the only one. But sometimes my workers come in if they want to speak with me privately.

Since there was no evidence that the back door

was broken into, police reasoned the burglary was an inside job.

They believed that one of Hopp's workers could have hidden in the store before closing. Then, when the owner locked the store for the night, the thief came out of hiding. He had the store all to himself.

Inside the office wastebasket, near the safe, police discovered a half-eaten sandwich.

The sandwich was sent to the crime lab for examination. A slice of cheese from the sandwich revealed important evidence. There were unusual teeth marks made by the person biting into it.

The police lab report is shown in EXHIBIT C.

The bite marks revealed that the person eating the sandwich had a center tooth missing. It showed the width of his front teeth and the spaces between them.

The teeth marks from the cheese were compared with those of the people who worked in the store. Andrew Turner's teeth marks matched exactly.

His middle tooth is missing and all other teeth matched the marks in the cheese.

On this basis, Andrew Turner was placed under arrest and is on trial here today.

Turner had worked for Mr. Hopp for seven months. But recently there was friction between them. It seemed Turner loved to eat. He constantly nibbled on store food without paying for it.

The State questioned Andrew Turner about his eating habits:

"Food? Sure I love food. Anyone can see that. Just look at the size of my stomach. I love to nibble.

"But I hate tomatoes. I'm allergic to them. Every time I eat a tomato my eyes get watery and I break out in a rash."

The defendant was asked to account for the half-eaten sandwich found in the wastebasket. The following is from his testimony:

"I admit it. That's the sandwich I ate. But I didn't eat it the night of the burglary. I got hungry in the late afternoon. I know Mr. Hopp doesn't like me eating. So I sneaked in his office while he was in the front of the store and gobbled up a fantastic sandwich. When I saw Hopp coming, I tossed the last of it in his wastebasket."

Andrew Turner's lawyer claims that at the time the safe alarm rang, Andrew was at home talking on the telephone to his girlfriend, Nancy King.

Nancy King supported the defendant's story. Miss King said they talked on the phone for about a half hour, although she was not sure of the exact time of the call.

Andrew Turner's lawyer claims that the testimony of Andrew's girlfriend provides the defendant with an alibi. And since Turner is allergic to tomatoes, it is further proof of his innocence.

LADIES AND GENTLEMEN OF THE JURY:
You have just heard the Case of the Squished Tomatoes. You must decide the merits of the State's accusation. Be sure to carefully examine the evidence in EXHIBITS A, B, and C.

Did Andrew Turner steal the money from the Hopp-n-Shop's safe? Or was he innocent?

EXHIBIT A

D.D. 8

| POLICE DEPARTMENT BURGLAR ALARM REPORT | PRECINCT 18th |
| | REPORT NUMBER 842A |

DATE June 5, 1989

TIME 9:56 pm

LOCATION Hopp-n-Shopp Grocery Store
82 Prospect St.

Police car #6 dispatched.

Monique Vespucci

OFFICER ON DUTY

EXHIBIT C

EXHIBIT C

EVIDENCE
SANDWICH
DATE RECIEVED
June 5, 1989
DATE ANALYZED
June 6, 1989

POLICE DEPARTMENT LABORATORY REPORT

REFERENCE
Hopp-n-Shopp
Grocery Store
82 Prospect St.

REPORT ON PARTIAL SANDWICH
FOUND IN WASTEBASKET

CONTENTS OF SANDWICH

Sandwich contained cheese, ham,
onions, hot green peppers, cucumbers
on white bread. Thick layer of
catsup on upper slice of bread.

DESCRIPTION OF BITE MARKS

Teeth marks in cheese reveal
the following:
Upper left central incisor missing
(#9). Malocclusion of upper left
first bicuspid (#13). Other teeth
of normal size.

Harry Whitcomb, Ph.D.
LABORATORY DIRECTOR

44

VERDICT

ANDREW TURNER BROKE INTO THE SAFE.

Turner testified that he couldn't be the burglar because he was allergic to tomatoes. In EXHIBIT C, the lab report describes the sandwich Turner was eating. It was topped with *catsup*. Turner admitted it was his sandwich, but forgot that catsup is made from tomatoes. Andrew Turner really wasn't allergic to tomatoes.
It was Turner who opened the safe and scrawled the sign on the mirror.

The Case of the
Missing Talk-Show Host

LADIES AND GENTLEMEN OF THE JURY:

Kidnapping is a serious crime in which someone carries away and holds a person against his or her will.

Since we are in criminal court today, the State is the accuser. The State charges Rudy Reddy, the owner of Reddy Roofing Company, with kidnapping Edward "Action" Jackson. Mr. Reddy, the defendant, says he was never involved in the kidnapping. Furthermore, he thinks the kidnapping was a fake.

Edward Jackson has testified as follows:

"Hello, everybody! This is Edward 'Action' Jackson, your WZDB Action Man, here to answer all your phone calls about... Oh, I'm sorry, sometimes I get a little carried away. Let me start again.

"My name is Edward Jackson. I'm the Action Man on radio station WZDB. My program is a telephone call-in show that gives advice to callers about practically anything.

"On my radio program of October 24, I received a phone call from Mrs. Betty Harcourt. Mrs. Harcourt complained that she had paid Reddy Roofing Company to have her roof repaired. But the roof still leaked and the company refused to fix it.

"I suggested that she place the following sign on her front lawn:

MY ROOF WAS POORLY REPAIRED BY

REDDY ROOFING COMPANY

AND IT STILL LEAKS!

Jackson's advice worked. The first day the sign was up, Rudy Reddy immediately went to Mrs. Harcourt's house to repair the roof. But because of the publicity, Reddy's business fell off badly. He was angry at Edward Jackson.

One morning, about a week after the radio program, a note appeared in the mailbox of station WZDB.

The note is entered as EXHIBIT A. It states that Edward Jackson had been kidnapped and would be returned only if $50,000 were paid in ransom.

When the radio station owner, Rhonda Braver, received the ransom note, she decided not to contact the police. Instead, she withdrew money from the bank and dropped it off at the location specified in the note.

The following afternoon, Edward Jackson walked into the radio station. It was three days after the alleged kidnapping. His suit was wrinkled and dirty. There was a bump on his head.

Jackson said he had escaped. He had been held in the woods inside a shed that was a mile from the radio station.

Police went to the location where the ransom money was placed. The money was still there. The kidnapper never picked it up.

Mr. Jackson described to the court how he was kidnapped:

"After my radio show Monday evening, I went to the parking lot to get my car. It was pretty dark out.

"As I opened the car door, someone grabbed me from behind. He covered my mouth and hit me on the head. I must have fainted.

"When I woke up, I found myself tied to a chair with a bandana over my eyes. I managed to loosen it by rubbing it against my shoulder. I found myself in a dark shed. No one was around.

"My head was throbbing with pain. I must have been unconscious for a long time. I felt tired and dirty. I hadn't washed or brushed my teeth for days. I was starved.

"It took some time, but I was able to untie the knots that bound me to the chair. Then I escaped."

EXHIBIT B is a photograph of Edward Jackson taken when police arrived at the radio station.

The police crime lab analyzed the black smudges on Jackson's face and clothing. They found it was a tar used for roof repair. On the strength of this evidence, Rudy Reddy was arrested.

The lawyer for the defendant admits that Reddy was very upset with Jackson. But he states that his client had nothing to do with the kidnapping.

He believes the kidnapping was actually a fake.

He points to the police report, EXHIBIT C. When Jackson returned to the radio station, he still had his wristwatch and wallet. Rudy Reddy's lawyer says that if Edward Jackson really had been kidnapped, his valuables would have been taken.

Mr. Reddy's lawyer continued:

"The popularity of Edward Jackson's radio show had been slipping badly. It was once the most-listened-to show on radio. But in recent months a quiz show on another station was attracting his audience.

"Jackson's kidnapping made the front page of the local newspaper. Everyone talked about it.

"It was great publicity for him. His popularity began to rise again after the kidnapping. More people than ever began listening to his show."

The lawyer for the defense states that Edward Jackson purposely faked the kidnapping for the publicity.

LADIES AND GENTLEMEN OF THE JURY:
You have just heard the Case of the Missing

Talk-Show Host. You are to decide the merit of the State's accusation. Be sure to carefully examine the evidence in EXHIBITS A, B, and C.

Did Rudy Reddy kidnap Edward Jackson? Or was the incident a publicity stunt?

EXHIBIT C

D.D. 12

CRIME CLASSIFICATION	POLICE DEPARTMENT SUPPLEMENTARY REPORT	PRECINCT
KIDNAPPING		12th
DATE		REPORT NUMBER
November 4, 1988		296-c

The officers below arrived at radio station WZDB at 1:37 pm. The station owner, Rhonda Braver, reported that one of her employees, Edward "Action" Jackson had been kidnapped on November 1 and had found his way back to the radio station.

Jackson's forehead had a bruise upper right and he was disheveled. His wallet and wristwatch were in his possession. No valuables were taken.

Braver claims a $50,000 ransom was paid. Braver and Jackson were taken to police headquarters for further questioning.

Fred Hargrove
OFFICER

M. Bogent
OFFICER

VERDICT

THE KIDNAPPING WAS A FAKE.

Jackson had been missing for three days. He testified he was tired and dirty. EXHIBIT B is a photograph of Jackson when he walked into the radio station, after his escape.

Despite the smudges on his face, Jackson didn't have a three-day beard. *He must have shaved.*

Edward Jackson faked the kidnapping and hid at home. He made himself up to look as though he had escaped from the shed. But he forgot about the beard.

The Case of
the Nosy Neighbor

Ladies and gentlemen of the jury:

All of us have the right to personal privacy. When we are in our homes we should be protected from nosy neighbors.

The residents of Freemont Terrace are in court today and have charged Penny Parker with snooping and interfering with their right to privacy. Ms. Parker, the defendant, says she is only interested in her neighbors' welfare and never bothers them.

Gordon Winslow of Freemont Terrace has testified as follows:

"Uhhh ... my name is Gordon ... Gordon Winslow. I'm a little nervous ... I've never been in a courtroom before. I live on Freemont Terrace.

"Freemont Terrace is a quiet little street lined with small houses. Most of us residents have lived there for years. We're quiet people.

"Eight months ago, Penny Parker moved into the neighborhood. She recently had retired from her job.

"She didn't make any friends. But everyone on

Freemont Terrace knew she was there. She often sat by her living room window watching her neighbors come and go. No matter where we went, Penny Parker was watching us."

Soon after Penny Parker moved in, people found mysterious letters in their mailboxes.

One homeowner received a note saying he should cut his grass more often. Another was told to keep the lid on her garbage can because it smelled.

One weekend, Gordon Winslow was sitting by his fireplace watching a soccer game on TV. During a commercial break, he went to the kitchen to fix a snack.

As he opened the refrigerator door, Winslow heard a noise outside his kitchen window. He turned around and saw a person's outline behind his window shade. Beneath it, a pair of binoculars was peering in at him.

EXHIBIT A is a view of the window from Winslow's kitchen.

Gordon Winslow ran outside, but by that time the intruder was gone.

He searched the area. In the flower bed below the window he found a handkerchief. On it were the initials "PP."

Mr. Winslow immediately took a photograph to show where the hanky was found. This photograph is entered in evidence as EXHIBIT B.

Gordon Winslow was very annoyed. He met with

neighbors and they voted to take legal action against Penny Parker. They have asked the court to order the defendant to stop bothering them.

Mr. Winslow testified as follows. First the question and then his answer:

Q: Did you recognize the person at the window?

A: No, I didn't. The shade was down, except for a space at the bottom. All I could see was an outline and a pair of binoculars.

Q: Why do you believe it was Ms. Parker?

A: It was definitely an outline of a woman's head. It must have been her. She's a terrible busybody. She knows when you're going to sneeze even before you do.

Q: What time did you go into your kitchen?

A: It was around 2:30 in the afternoon.

Q: How do you know the hanky hadn't been lying there for days?

A: I was puttering in my yard that morning and cleaned out the flower bed. It wasn't there then.

Penny Parker says that her neighbor is mistaken. She never peeked through Gordon Winslow's window. She testified as follows:

"I wish the people of Freemont Terrace would understand I'm only looking out for their own good.

"Many of them work. They should be glad to

have a nice person like me watching out for the neighborhood."

Penny Parker says the hanky was hers and she could explain how it got there:

"I was taking my daily walk along a path that cuts through the rear of Freemont Terrace. It was around noon. It was cold out and a strong wind was blowing. I was wearing my coat and hat.

"All of a sudden a gust of wind blew my hat off and into Mr. Winslow's yard. So I ran after it.

"My hat landed in his flower bed. I picked it up and went on my way. The hanky must have fallen out of my pocket."

EXHIBIT C is the hanky found by Mr. Winslow and which the defendant identifies as hers.

Penny Parker continued her testimony:

"I never looked into his window. It must have been someone else. I was home at 2:30 when Winslow said it happened. I may be interested in my neighbors' welfare. But I'm not *that* kind of person."

Penny Parker asks that the action against her be dismissed. She likes her neighbors and says they are mistaken to think she is nosy.

LADIES AND GENTLEMEN OF THE JURY: You have just heard the Case of the Nosy Neighbor. You must decide the merits of the claim against Penny Parker. Be sure to carefully examine the evidence in EXHIBITS A, B, and C.

Was Penny Parker the nosy neighbor who peeked into Gordon Winslow's kitchen window? Or was it someone else?

EXHIBIT A

EXHIBIT C

VERDICT

PENNY PARKER WAS THE NOSY NEIGHBOR.

In her testimony, Ms. Parker said she had dropped the hanky when her hat blew into Winslow's flower bed earlier that day.

But the chimney smoke in EXHIBIT B shows that the wind was blowing *away* from Winslow's house. Therefore, Parker's hat could not have been blown into the flower bed. It would have blown in the opposite direction.

Penny Parker made up the story to explain how the hanky got there.

The Case of
the Hotel Break-in

LADIES AND GENTLEMEN OF THE JURY:

If a hotel provides a safety deposit box for guests, it is not responsible for property that is stolen from their rooms. But if a hotel worker steals the property, that may be a different matter.

That is the point of law you must keep in mind today as you decide whether an employee was responsible for a hotel theft.

Donna Smith, the plaintiff, is a traveling salesperson for the Vega Jewelry Company. She is suing the Erbamont Hotel. She claims that while she was in the lobby, one of the hotel's workers stole a jewelry case from her hotel room.

The lawyer for the hotel claims the theft was not done by a hotel worker. He believes that when Donna Smith discovered her jewelry case had been stolen, she made it look like a hotel worker was responsible, so she could sue the hotel.

Donna Smith has testified as follows:

"My name is Donna Smith. I'm a sales representative for Vega Jewelry. On the afternoon of Thursday, October 21, I checked into the Erbamont Hotel. When I got to my room, I saw a notice on the wall that said:

THIS HOTEL DOES NOT ACCEPT LIABILITY FOR LOSS OR DAMAGE TO GUESTS' PROPERTY. VALUABLES MAY BE STORED IN SAFETY DEPOSIT BOXES AT THE FRONT DESK.

"I carry a lot of valuable jewelry samples with me so I went right back down to the front desk to find out about a safety deposit box. I left my jewelry case in my room."

When Smith returned to her room she took a nap. Upon waking, she discovered her case was gone. It contained more than $25,000 in jewelry samples.

I will now quote from the testimony of Ms. Smith. First the question and then her answer:

Q: What floor was your hotel room on?

A: On the sixth floor, next to the housekeeping closet. I think that's where the hotel's sheets and towels are stored.

Q: Can you describe the layout of your hotel room?

A: The door to my room opens onto the hallway. But the room has an extra door. That door goes into the housekeeping closet.

EXHIBIT A is a diagram of the sixth floor. Note the hallway door to Smith's room and the side door between her room and the housekeeping closet.

Donna Smith continued her testimony:

Q: Can your room be entered from that housekeeping closet?

A: No. There is a bolt on the door. It can only be unlocked from inside my room.

Q: What happened after you returned from the front desk?

A: I went to my room and took a quick nap. When I woke up I looked around for my jewelry case. I couldn't believe it was missing.

When the police arrived they discovered that someone had punched a hole in the side door of Donna Smith's hotel room right near the bolt. A wire had been inserted into the hole.

Donna Smith's lawyer described how the theft occurred. He explained that only hotel workers had a key to the closet. He believes that one of them entered the housekeeping closet, punched out the hole, inserted a wire, and slipped it around the bolt in Smith's room. The intruder then pulled the bolt open and entered the room.

EXHIBIT B is a photograph of the hole and wire as seen from Smith's room.

Donna Smith's lawyer also has entered as evidence EXHIBIT C. It is a photograph of the door as seen from inside the housekeeping closet. The blurred fingerprints on the door show where the thief punched out the hole.

The hotel's lawyer acknowledges that the jewelry was stolen. But she claims it was not an employee who stole it.

The lawyer believes that while Smith was at the front desk, an unknown thief was able to break into her room through the main hallway door. The thief took the jewelry and fled.

In his testimony, Dudley Nelson, the hotel manager, explained his version of the robbery. First the question and then his answer:

Q: What makes you think Donna Smith altered the evidence to make it look like a hotel worker committed the theft?

A: It has to do with the time after Ms. Smith left the front desk. She didn't report the robbery for nearly half an hour. She said she took a nap before she discovered the theft, but I don't believe her.

Q: Why do you think she waited so long?

A: When she saw the jewelry was missing, she thought up a plan to blame someone from the hotel. Smith slipped out of the hotel and bought tools from a nearby hardware store. Then she returned to her room and made the hole.

Erbamont Hotel stands by its explanation. It

believes the theft was committed by an outsider and the hotel is not responsible for the stolen jewelry.

LADIES AND GENTLEMEN OF THE JURY: You have just heard the Case of the Hotel Break-in. You must decide the merits of Donna Smith's evidence in EXHIBITS A, B, and C.

Did a hotel worker break into the plaintiff's room? Or did Donna Smith make it look that way?

EXHIBIT A

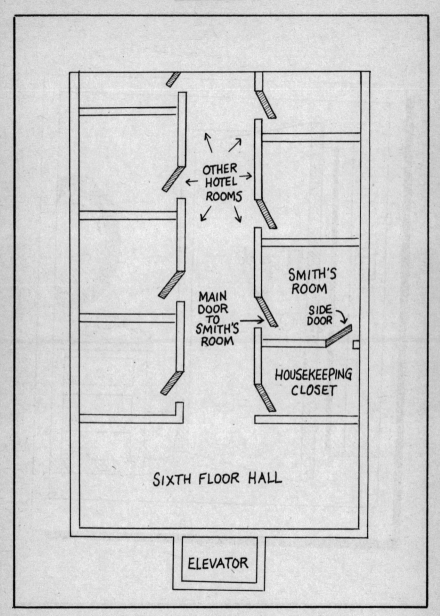

OTHER HOTEL ROOMS

SMITH'S ROOM

MAIN DOOR TO SMITH'S ROOM

SIDE DOOR

HOUSEKEEPING CLOSET

SIXTH FLOOR HALL

ELEVATOR

EXHIBIT C

VERDICT

A HOTEL WORKER BROKE INTO
THE ROOM.

The hole in the door was made from inside the housekeeping closet. The edges of a hole made in wood on the side where a sharp tool enters the wood will be smooth. But the edges will be rough on the opposite side where the tool punctures through.

In EXHIBIT B, the rough and splintered edges around the hole are inside Donna Smith's room. On the opposite side of the door in EXHIBIT C, the edges are smooth.

If Smith had made the hole, the splinters would have appeared on the opposite side of the door.

The Case of
the Barking Dog

LADIES AND GENTLEMEN OF THE JURY:

The owner of a pet must make sure that his or her animal behaves. If a pet damages someone's property, the owner is expected to pay. However, there must be proof that the animal actually caused the damage.

Please keep this issue of proof in mind as you decide the case before you today.

Ann Potter, the plaintiff, has charged that Norma Winkler's terrier injured her pet goose and caused other damage. Norma Winkler, the defendant, says that Mrs. Potter is mistaken. The injury was caused by a wild raccoon.

For her birthday present, Mrs. Winkler's husband surprised her with a pet terrier. She named the dog "Lady."

Ann Potter has testified as follows:

"My name is Ann Potter and I just love animals, don't you? But my most favorite animals are geese. I just go 'ga-ga' for geese. I have four geese that

I've raised in my backyard, and I sell baby geese, which are called goslings, for pets.

"On the afternoon of July 8, I was in my bedroom and heard some noises in the backyard. My geese were honking and I heard the loud barking of a dog.

"I hurried downstairs. The yard was empty. Then I ran over to the cage where I keep my four geese.

"There was Hugo lying on the ground. He was badly hurt. Hugo's leg was broken and his tail feathers were missing. The feathers were scattered all over the yard.

"Then I knew why I had heard a dog barking. It was Norma Winkler's pet terrier, Lady, who was responsible."

On a wooden table in a corner of the cage, Mrs. Potter kept her geese's eggs. The eggs were on the ground, all of them broken.

EXHIBIT A is a photograph of the broken eggs.

Mrs. Potter is suing for the money she paid the veterinarian to fix Hugo's leg. She claims she also is owed $50 for the broken eggs that were knocked over by Lady. When the eggs hatched she could have sold the goslings for $5.00 each.

Ann Potter was questioned by Norma Winkler's lawyer. First the question and then her answer:

Q: Did you actually see Lady in your yard?
A: No. But I'd recognize her bark anywhere. It was definitely Lady's barking. My geese get

excited when they're scared. They start to honk.

Q: Did you see any other animals in your yard? For instance, did you see a raccoon?

A: No. I can't see the cage from my bedroom window.

Q: When you ran into your yard, did you see Lady?

A: The yard was empty. I must have scared Lady off. She probably slipped through the hole in my fence.

EXHIBIT B is a photograph of the hole in Mrs. Potter's backyard fence where the dog could have entered.

Norma Winkler insists that it wasn't Lady who did the damage. But she admits that Lady was in her neighbor's yard earlier on the day that the damage occurred.

Mrs. Winkler testified as follows:

"I let Lady outside every morning and watch her from my doorway. She's well trained, you know.

"That morning I saw Lady run over to Ann Potter's house. I chased after her, but she slipped through the hole in the Potters' fence. I called Lady and she came back out and jumped into my arms. She was only in the yard for a minute."

Mrs. Winkler stated that there was a wild raccoon in the neighborhood that probably caused the damage Ann Potter blamed on Lady.

She continued her testimony:

"Later that day, at the time Ann Potter's geese were honking, I was walking Lady past her house. I remember thinking that there must have been a raccoon in the Potters' yard. Lady always barks when she smells a raccoon.

"The barking Ann Potter heard was from Lady, all right. But I was walking her on a leash outside the Potters' house.

"Mrs. Potter phoned me when she found her goose was injured. She yelled at me over the phone, using terrible language.

"When she hung up I went into her backyard. I saw animal tracks in the yard. One set were the tracks Lady had made when she ran there and back earlier that morning.

"But I saw some other prints that looked like they could have been a raccoon's. So I hurried home and brought back my camera. I took a picture of the prints."

This photograph is entered as EXHIBIT C. Note the four-pointed prints that Norma Winkler admits are Lady's. The darker five-pointed prints are those of another animal, possibly a raccoon.

Norma Winkler continued her testimony:

"You see those prints? A raccoon could have easily gone through the fence and attacked the geese. How can Ann Potter say it was my dog? She can't make me pay for the damage because

Lady wasn't responsible. My Lady is a lady!"

LADIES AND GENTLEMEN OF THE JURY:
You have just heard the Case of the Barking Dog. You must decide the merits of Ann Potter's claim. Be sure to carefully examine the evidence in EXHIBITS A, B, and C.

Was Lady responsible for the backyard damage? Or did a wild raccoon do it?

EXHIBIT C

VERDICT

A RACCOON DID THE DAMAGE.

In EXHIBIT C, one of the dark five-pointed prints of the raccoon is on top of a crushed feather. This means the raccoon stepped on Hugo's feather *after* he had lost his tail. One of the prints of Lady is underneath a feather. Lady must have left the yard *before* Hugo lost his tail feathers.

81

The Case of
the Filbert Flub

LADIES AND GENTLEMEN OF THE JURY:

When a person obtains something valuable by means of trickery, it is the same as stealing.

Keep this in mind as you decide the case before you today.

Otis Oats, the plaintiff, is suing his neighbor Brad Sweeny for tricking him into giving up a rare postage stamp. Brad Sweeny, the defendant, claims that Oats is mistaken. The rare stamp had been in his collection for years.

Otis Oats has testified as follows:

"I had just returned from visiting my Aunt Emma in Urbanville. She gave me an old family chest to keep. It had lots of old letters and postcards in it.

"When I got home, I looked through the chest. The stamps on the envelopes seemed kind of unusual. I thought some might be valuable. That's when I phoned Brad. His hobby is stamp collecting. It all started when his grandmother gave him her collection years ago. I figured if anyone would know about my stamps, it would be Brad."

The two friends went through the envelopes. After examining them carefully, Brad Sweeny told Oats the stamps weren't worth any more than they had been the day they were printed.

Otis Oats continued his testimony:

"I was disappointed. I told Brad to help himself to any stamps he wanted. He took an envelope that had a stamp with a picture of Filmore Filbert, the inventor of the supernail."

Several months later, Otis Oats read in a newspaper that Sweeny had sold his entire stamp collection, including a very rare stamp worth thousands of dollars. The newspaper had a picture of this stamp.

Oats was very upset. The stamp looked exactly like the one he had given Brad Sweeny, and which Sweeny had told him was worthless.

The envelope with the stamp attached, which Oats says he gave to Sweeny, has been entered as EXHIBIT A.

The Filmore Filbert stamp is known by collectors as the "Filbert flub." When it was originally printed, the artist accidentally drew an extra finger on Filbert's left hand.

The mistake was quickly caught, the hand redrawn, and new stamps printed. But some "Filbert flubs" were already in circulation. Today the "Filbert flub" is very valuable.

A close-up of this rare stamp appears as EXHIBIT B. Filmore Filbert is pictured holding his supernail, a nail that can be hammered into anything. You will note the six fingers on Filbert's left hand.

Otis Oats explained to the court why he is certain the rare stamp is his:

"I visited Brad Sweeny's house lots of times. He was proud of his stamp collection and he always showed it to me. In fact, I got a little bored from seeing it so much. But Brad never showed me the "Filbert flub" stamp. If it were so valuable, he would have been proud to show it to me."

Otis Oats claims that Brad Sweeny took the envelope he gave him with the "Filbert flub" stamp and erased the address. Over it, Sweeny wrote the name and address of his own grandmother, Nora Sweeny. That way Sweeny could say the letter with the rare stamp was addressed to her.

Brad Sweeny says that Otis Oats is mistaken. He explained to the court how he got the rare stamp:

"That's my grandmother's name and address on the envelope. She gave it to me. Grandma was a serious stamp collector. She began collecting in 1920, when she was only ten years old. She was even written up in the newspapers."

Brad Sweeny showed as EXHIBIT C an article describing his grandmother's collection.

A crime lab expert was called in to examine the envelope with the stamp. A special method of chemical analysis was used. Because the envelope was very old, the laboratory expert was unsure whether the original name and address were erased.

Brad Sweeny continued his testimony:

"Even if there were eraser marks, it doesn't prove anything. The letter was addressed in pencil and the person sending it to my grandmother could have made a mistake in her address, erased it, and corrected the mistake."

LADIES AND GENTLEMEN OF THE JURY:

You have just heard the Case of the Filbert Flub. You must decide the merits of Otis Oats's claim. Be sure to carefully examine the evidence in EXHIBITS A, B, and C.

Was the stamp that Brad Sweeny sold from his own collection? Or was it the stamp Otis Oats gave him?

EXHIBIT A

EXHIBIT C

LIBRARY FEATURES STAMP COLLECTION

NORA SWEENY

The Madison Public Library will have an exhibit of the stamp collection of local resident Mrs. Nora Sweeny.

Her collection includes hundreds of unusual stamps, including several that are quite rare.

Mrs. Sweeny has been collecting stamps since she was a youngster.

"I got interested in stamps when I was ten years old, some thirty years ago," said Sweeny. "The library asked if they could be displayed for the townsfolk to see. I think it's a wonderful idea."

Mrs. Sweeny has shown her collection at many antiquarian exhibits in the state.

Library hours are 9 a.m. to 5 p.m. Closed on Sundays.

VERDICT

SWEENY TRICKED OATS INTO GIVING HIM THE STAMP.

The envelope with the Fillmore Filbert stamp in EXHIBIT A is addressed to Sweeny's grandmother, Mrs. Nora Sweeny. The date on the envelope shows it was mailed in 1920.

But Sweeny testified that his grandmother began collecting stamps in 1920 when she was only ten years old.

That means Nora was ten years old when the letter was mailed. She wouldn't have been a "Mrs." then, and she would have had her unmarried last name.

Brad Sweeny erased the name on the envelope Otis Oats gave him and substituted his grandmother's name. But he forgot she was too young to be Mrs. Nora Sweeny.